WORKING WORDS

ou.
the
hat
ms.

1. Use this to climb: __ ADD __ __

2. Extra, leftover: __ __ __PLUS

3. Something taught in school: LESS __ __

4. Word spoken by a raven in a famous poem: __ __ __ __ __MORE

5. Payment earned on an investment: DIVIDE __ __

6. Every now and then: __ __ __ __ TIMES

7. Have more people than the opposition: __ __ __ NUMBER

8. Make an original picture or pattern: __ __ SIGN

9. Go out of whack: __ __ __ FUNCTION

10. Sale price: __ __ __ COUNT

11. Work together to reach a goal: __ __ __ __ __ RATE

12. Person who comes to live permanently in a new country: SET __ __ __ __

Illustration: Randy Llewellyn

Answer on page 48

DRAGON AROUND

These dancing dragons are being prepared for the big parade. Each red section requires two people to move the dragon, each blue

Answer on page 48

section requires three people, and each head requires one person. Can you figure out which dragon needs the most people?

CARD QUEST
Each suit of cards is missing a number from 1 to 9. Write the missing number in the space next to the right suit. The right answer will give you the year that Delaware became the first of the United States.
♥____ ♦____ ♣____ ♠____
Answer on page 48
Illustration: Judith Hunt
Hint on page 46
6 MATHMANIA

Answer on page 48

BE SEATED

Can you help find the seat where each person belongs? Look at the tickets. The top letter and number pair shows which ticket matches each seat. Write the bottom letter

in the proper seat. If you do this correctly, you'll find a hidden message when you read the letters you've written from left to right and top to bottom.

Answer on page 48

TAKE-OUT SERVICE

Subtract the number of mints, cookies, or other extras on each tray from the number on the bag. Put the solution on each bill so our delivery person knows how much to collect.

Illustration: Jason Thorne

Answer on page 48

COLOR BY NUMBERS

Don't get dizzy as you go around trying to find what's waiting here. Use the key to color in the spaces with the matching number of dots.

KEY

1 dot — Light Blue	4 dots — Yellow
2 dots — Dark Blue	5 dots — Brown
3 dots — Green	6 dots — Gray

Illustration: Rob Sepanak

Answer on page 48

DOT'S THE ANSWER

To discover the answers to three fast facts, you'll have to be quick. Count the dots described in each statement to find out what number belongs in the blank.

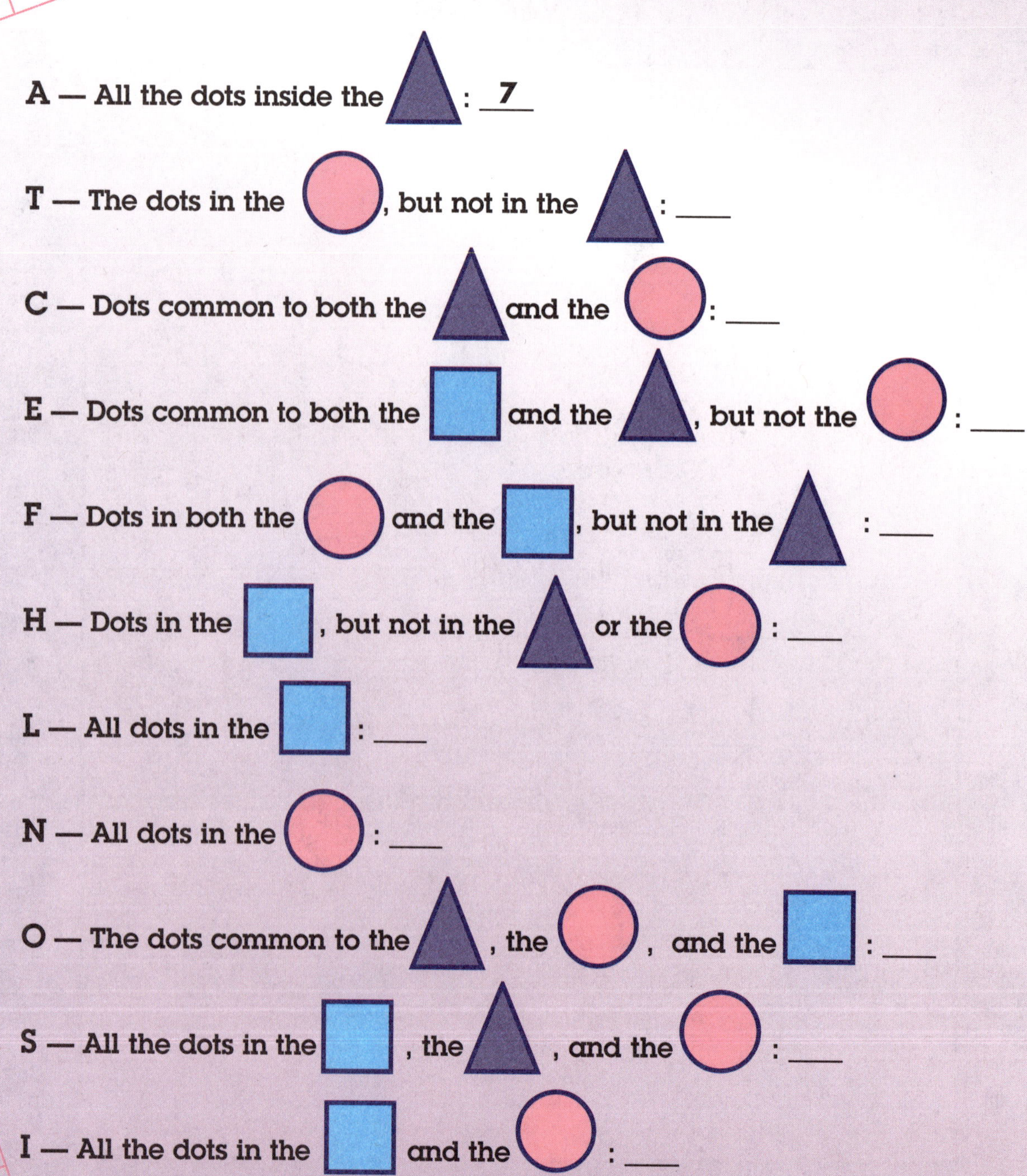

A — All the dots inside the : 7

T — The dots in the , but not in the : ___

C — Dots common to both the and the : ___

E — Dots common to both the and the , but not the : ___

F — Dots in both the and the , but not in the : ___

H — Dots in the , but not in the or the : ___

L — All dots in the : ___

N — All dots in the : ___

O — The dots common to the , the , and the : ___

S — All the dots in the , the , and the : ___

I — All the dots in the and the : ___

Then match that number with the letter at the beginning of the statement. Write that letter in the space above the matching number. The first one has been done to start you off.

This is the fastest bird with speeds of more than 200 miles per hour:

___ A ___ ___ ___ ___.
4 7 13 2 1 8

This is the fastest land animal with speeds of up to 65 miles per hour:

___ ___ ___ ___ ___ A ___.
2 5 3 3 6 7 5

This is the fastest fish with speeds of up to 50 miles per hour:

___ A ___ ___ ___ ___ ___ ___.
18 7 16 13 4 16 18 5

Answer on page 48

PACK IT IN

Sidney the sign painter is headed for Australia. But before he can go anywhere, he must pack this last suitcase with the letters he needs to make a sign for FLETCHS. Can you get all the letters to fit within Sid's suitcase? Letters may be turned around, backward, and upside down, but no letters may overlap.

Illustration: R. Michael Palan

Hint on page 46

Answer on page 49

Answer on page 49

WINNING INNINGS

Uh-oh! At the bottom of the sixth inning, the scoreboard went on the blink! Now no one knows which team won the championship. Luckily, Rhonda Rewrite, the roving reporter, kept extensive notes on the

Hint on page 46

action. As the game moved into the seventh, Wilson's Wonders were ahead 5–3. Can you read the rest of Rhonda's report to tell this game's final score?

SEVENTH INNING

SALLY'S SLUGGERS

Batter #1. Double
Batter #2. Pop-out to the infield
Batter #3. Single. No runners advance.
Batter #4. Single
Batter #5. Strikeout
Batter #6. Double. Each runner advances two bases.
Batter #7. Pick-off at second

WILSON'S WONDERS

Batter #1. Strikeout
Batter #2. Triple
Batter #3. Single. Runner on third does not advance.
Batter #4. Single. Runner on third comes home.
Batter #5. Pop-out to catcher
Batter #6. Bunt for a single
Batter #7. Out at second

EIGHTH INNING

SALLY'S SLUGGERS

Batter #1. Walk
Batter #2. Strikeout
Batter #3. Single
Batter #4. Home run
Batter #5. Pop-out
Batter #6. Double
Batter #7. Out at first

WILSON'S WONDERS

Batter #1. Single
Batter #2. Walk
Batter #3. Strikeout
Batter #4. Strikeout
Batter #5. Single
Batter #6. Pop-out to left field

NINTH INNING

SALLY'S SLUGGERS

Batter #1. Triple
Batter #2. Strikeout
Batter #3. Fly-out to right, but runner on third tags up and beats the throw to the plate.
Batter #4. Single
Batter #5. Bunt for a single
Batter #6. Strikeout

WILSON'S WONDERS

Batter #1. Double
Batter #2. Strikeout
Batter #3. Walk
Batter #4. Double
Batter #5. Home run
Batter #6. Single
Batter #7. Single
Batter #8. Double play at first and second

Answer on page 49

Illustration: Marc Nadel

HONEYCOMB

Here's a sweet treat: Put the numbers from 1 to 7 into the cells of this honeycomb so that the numbers in each straight line of three cells equal 12. Each of the two side groups of three connected cells must also equal 12.

Hint on page 46

Answer on page 49

SWIMMING SEQUENCES

Bubbles O'Shea, the swim-team statistician, has noticed a pattern in the number of laps each swimmer swims during practice. Check out the number of laps for each day of the week, and see if you can tell how many laps each swimmer will swim on Friday.

Illustration: Bill Colrus

	Mon.	Tues.	Wed.	Thurs.	Fri.
Len Leakie	3	4	5	6	?
Ben Aquatik	5	6	5	6	?
Lily Padd	11	9	7	5	?
Clarence Clearwater	2	5	11	23	?
Mark Spritz	6	7	9	12	?
Sally Splash	4	9	5	10	?

Answer on page 49

DIGIT DOES IT

That super sleuth, Inspector Digit, has cracked another major case. After months of work, he's discovered the headquarters of a music-smuggling ring. He also found a coded message from the Audio Pirate to his crew.

Hint on page 47

Crack the code and give the Inspector a real clue to help him catch this disorderly recorder. Be sure to pick up the sixteen compact discs at the scene for evidence.

3 17 3 13 2' 21 1 18 9 22 22 1 4 13!

13 1 1 2 10 1 13 1 16 8 13?

2 10 1 21 3 4 1 11 7 4 2 10

3 13 15 3 18 18 2 4 1 3 13 9 4 1.

11 1 10 3 17 1 2 7 13 10 5 6

2 10 1 15 4 5 19 10 2 3 11 3 21.

22 4 5 14 19 2 10 1 8 5 13 16 13

2 7 2 10 1 11 1 13 2 13 5 8 1

8 7 16 20 13 3 2 15 5 8 14 5 19 10 2

12 4 5 8 3 21.

2 10 1 3 9 8 5 7 6 5 4 3 2 1

Illustration: John Nez

Answer on page 49

THE ISSUE AT HAND

Corey has a complete run of his favorite monthly comic book, *Protector-8*. He has issues 1 through 36. He's trying to remember the issue number in which each villain listed appeared. Use the clues to help him sort out the comics.

Answer on page 49

PLACES, EVERYONE

These whirling numbers are about to drop. It's up to you to put them in the right tubes. Look for the label on each number to guess the tube in which it belongs. The numbers in each tube will go from the largest number at the top to the smallest number at the bottom.

TEN THOUSANDS 3

TENS 4

HUNDREDS 2

TENS 3

100,000 10,000 1,000 100 10 1

Illustration: Cathy Pernice

Answer on page 50

SCRAMBLED PICTURE

Copy these mixed-up rectangles into the spaces on the next page. The letters and numbers tell

Illustration: Rob Sepanak

you where each piece belongs. The first one, A-3, has been done for you.

Answer on page 50

MATHMAGIC

Illustration: Marc Nadel

HOT AND COLD

Which thermometer belongs in each picture?

Illustration: Don Robison

Answer on page 50

GET THE PICTURE

While exploring the caves on the planet Gallopam, Sheryl stumbled across some pictographs created by an unknown cave painter. Pictographs use pictures

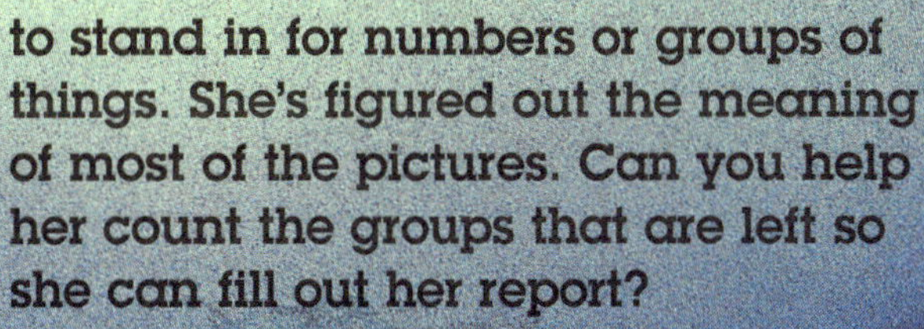

to stand in for numbers or groups of things. She's figured out the meaning of most of the pictures. Can you help her count the groups that are left so she can fill out her report?

= 5 creatures spotted

= 10 creatures spotted

Zoopnoodler

Ignoradon

Tricyclian

Frinkski

Allowichus

1. How many Zoopnoodlers did this cave painter see in a lifetime?
2. How many Frinkskis did this cave painter see in a lifetime?
3. How many Allowichus did this cave painter see in a lifetime?
4. How many Tricyclians did this cave painter see in a lifetime?
5. How many Ignoradons did this cave painter see in a lifetime?
6. Which animal was seen most often?
7. Which animal was seen least often?
8. How many more Ignoradons were seen than Allowichus?

Answer on page 50

Illustration: Michael Austin

PRECISE ICE

Can you trace this shape without crossing over or doubling back along any lines?

Answer on page 50

LIQUID FUN

Each tube is filled with a certain amount of liquid. Next to each tube is a small beaker. It's up to you to help Dr. Karloff figure out the number of times the large tube will fill up the small beaker.

MYSTERIOUS TIMES

The Arc of the Circle, a famous sculpture, was taken from the Math Museum. A security guard noticed the sculpture was missing when the museum closed at 5:00 p.m. The sculpture was last seen at 2:00 p.m. The local constable, Dave Iddidby, is on the case and has already

Hint on page 47

interviewed four suspects. He's also driven around town to check their stories. Using the map he made, he soon found out who had enough time to commit this crime. Can you follow his notes and check the map to nab his nefarious nemesis?

SUSPECTS

MATT E. MADDOX: I was at Flora's Flowers at 2:00 p.m. Then I went to Tippy's Canoes. After an hour, I went to the post office for 18 minutes. Then I went to Cleo's Clippers to pick up Cleo for dinner.

DEE VYDE: I left Cleo's Clippers at 2:00 p.m. and went to Tippy's Canoes. After canoeing for $2\frac{1}{2}$ hours, I was famished. I hurried to Ralph's Restaurant for an early dinner.

MAL T. PLICASHUN: I left the post office at 2:00 p.m. and went to the theater. I watched a movie that lasted 2 hours. After that, I had to go to the post office again. Then I went to Tippy's Canoes.

CAL Q. LATER: I left Ralph's Restaurant at 2:00 p.m. and went to the theater. After $1\frac{1}{2}$ hours, I remembered I left my hat at Ralph's, so I went back to get it. After that, I went to the post office.

Illustration: Scott Peck

Answer on page 50

TRY ANGLES

This time, Simone built a little too much. Can you remove three lines so that all the remaining lines will form three triangles?

Answer on page 50

SIDE ISSUE

Find a pentagon of five triangles with numbers that add up to 50. The five sides of the pentagon do not need to be the same length.

12	19	14	
3	10		2
5	13	3	4
7	9		11
8	15	16	

Answer on page 51

LUCKY DUCKS

What's the fewest ducks you would need to knock down in order to win each prize on the shelves? You must get an exact score to get a prize.

Answer on page 51

HEY! EMERGENCY LOCATION PUZZLE SYSTEM

A mystery city is located an exact distance from each of three cities listed. For example, the first mystery city is 267 miles from El Paso. The mystery city is also 139 miles from Gallup and 212 miles from Durango.

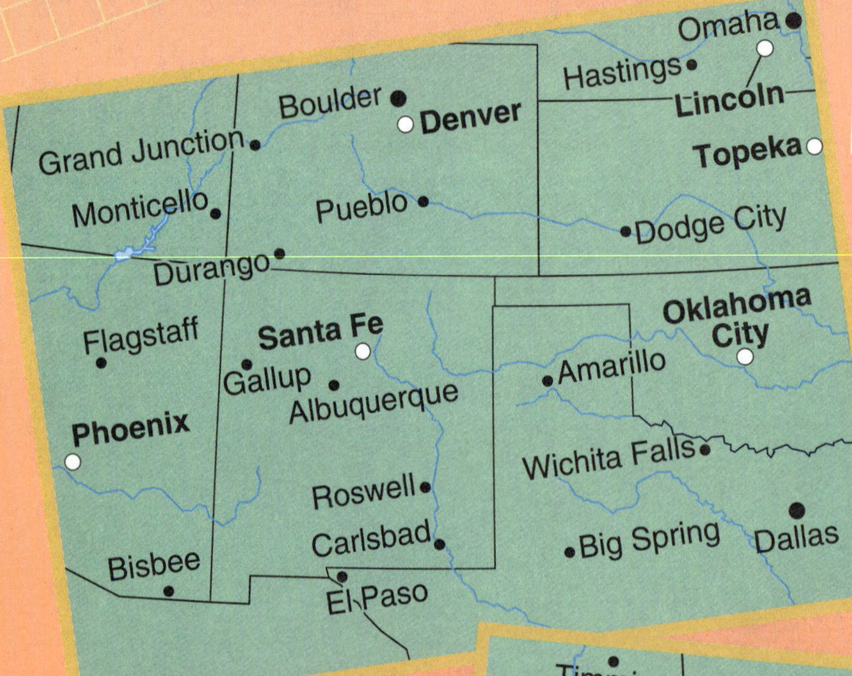

1. El Paso 267 miles
   Gallup 139 miles
   Durango 212 miles

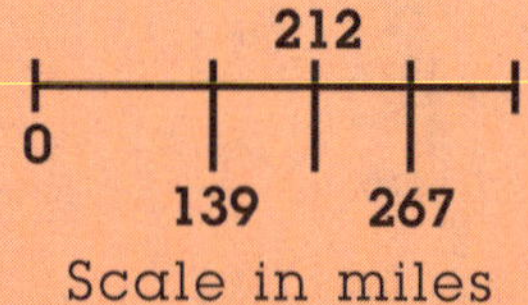

2. Albany 226 miles
   Ottawa 128 miles
   Bangor 290 miles

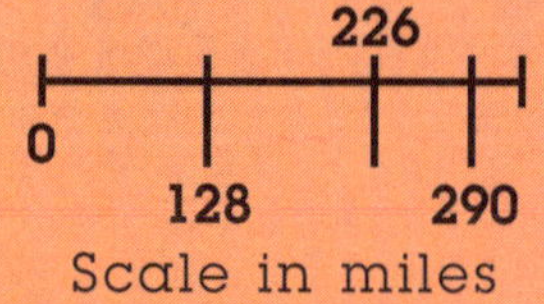

Hint on page 47

Answer on page 51

It's up to you to find where the three distances meet on each map. Put an X on the map where you think each mystery city is located.

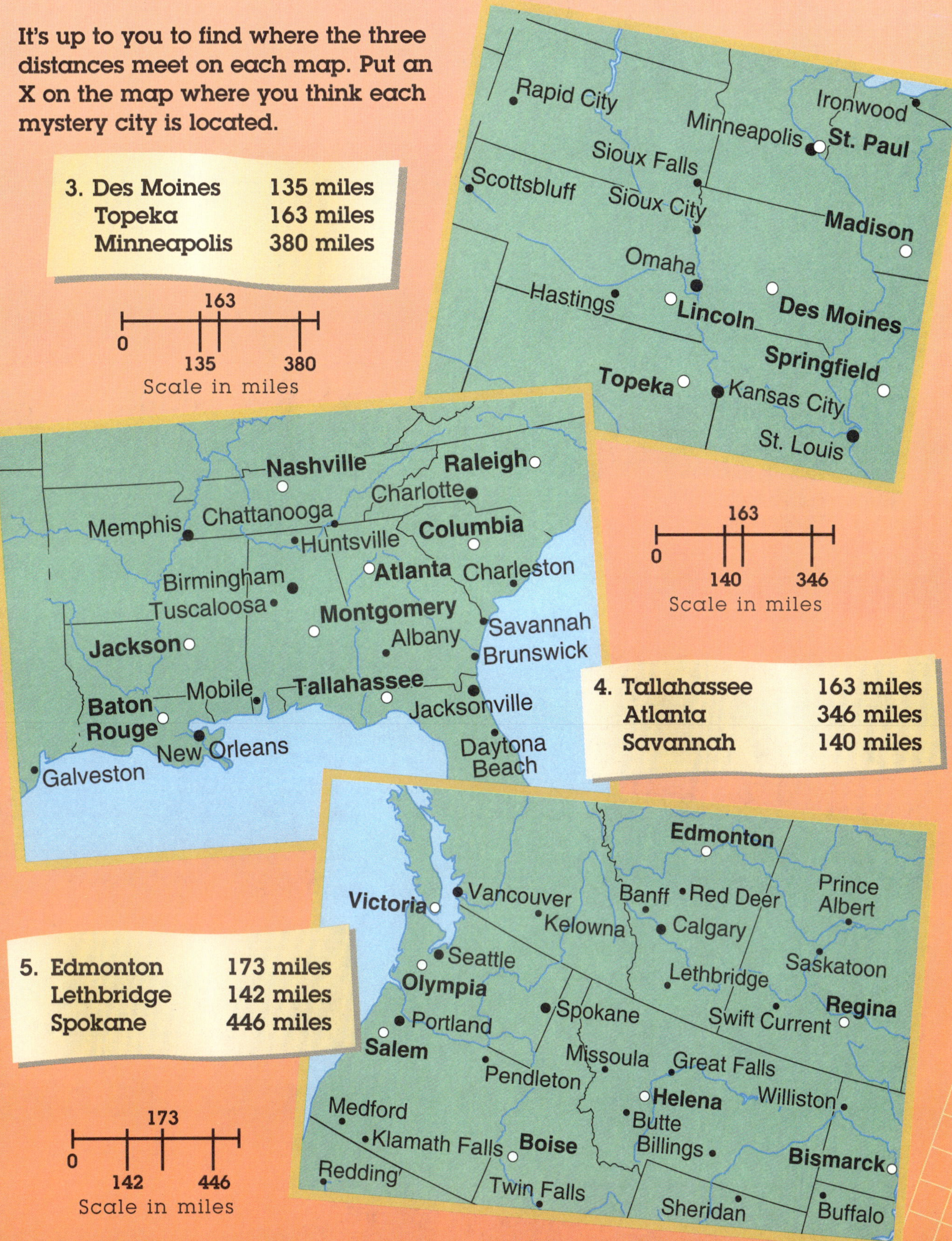

DROP EVERYTHING
To answer this riddle, solve each problem and then find the raindrop with the matching number. Put the letter beside each problem. Read the letters down to find the answer to the riddle.
W 15
K 12
Z 23
E 20
I 18
C 0
A 24
T 16
N 11
R 35
S 9
H 6
5 x 3 ___
2 x 9 ___
4 x 4 ___
6 x 1 ___
7 x 5 ___
3 x 8 ___
6 x 3 ___
11 x 1 ___
17 x 0 ___
2 x 3 ___
5 x 4 ___
8 x 0 ___
4 x 3 ___
9 x 1 ___
How does a weather forecaster pay his bills?
Answer on page 51
Illustration: Judith Hunt
40

DOTS A LOT

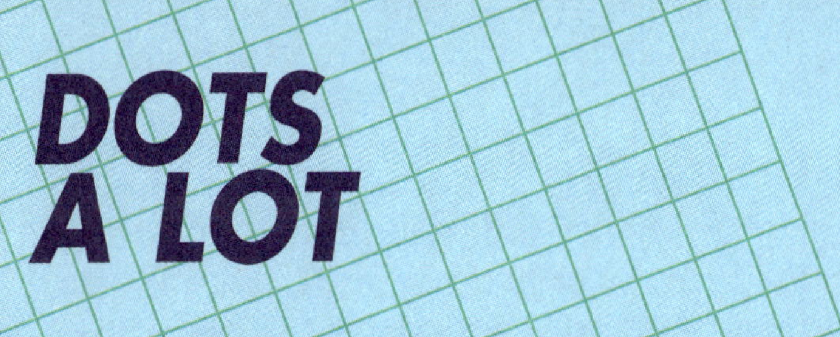

Be careful if you try to play this horn. Maybe you'd better just count by 2s to connect the dots, then get out of the way.

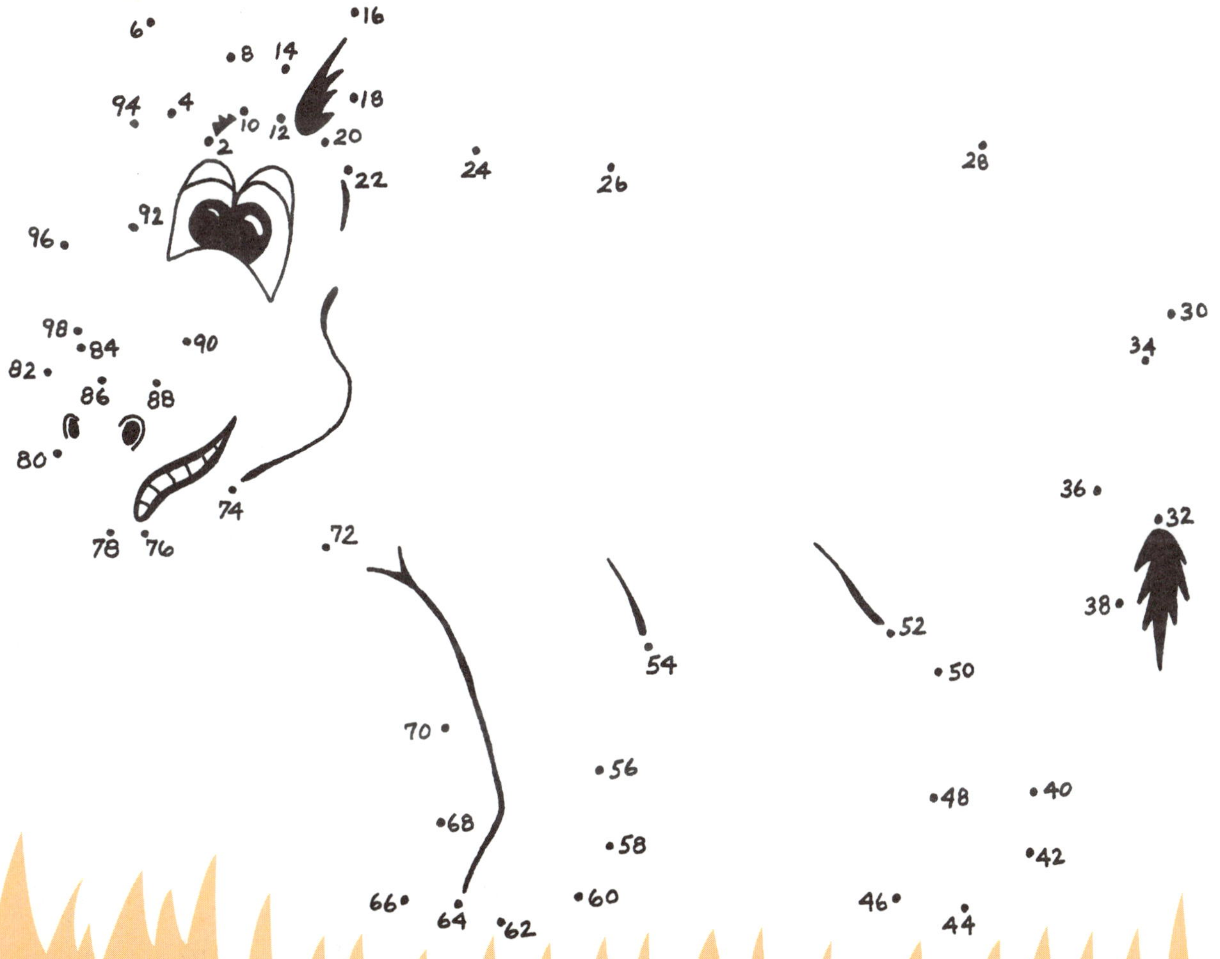

Illustration: Rob Sepanak

Answer on page 51

MONKEYING AROUND

Bungling Brothers Circus is trying to get new outfits for Sasha's Scintillating Simians. But first the monkeys and apes need to weigh in. Can you help Sasha figure

Illustration: David Helton

out how much each of his performers weigh? He knows that each bale of hay weighs four pounds and each bunch of bananas weighs three pounds.

Answer on page 51

BODY CODES

Our resident physician, Dr. Sue Cherr, is trying to bone up for a lecture she has to give. Her secretary typed up her

notes, but he left all the answers in a strange code. Can you use the key on his desk to crack the number needed in each case?

Answer on page 51

HINTS AND BRIGHT IDEAS

These hints may help with some of the trickier puzzles.

COVER

Add the weights of the boxes together until you have a total of 1,000 pounds. All but one box should make it in one trip.

CARD QUEST (page 6)

Count aces as ones.

BE SEATED (pages 8-9)

The top letter on the ticket tells you in which row the seat is located. Count the seats until you find the one with the same number that's on the ticket. The top left seat is F1. The ticket for F1 has a *W* on it. Write the *W* in the F1 seat. Continue until you find the message.

PACK IT IN (page 14)

Some of the letters will appear sideways or upside down. You may want to draw the letters on a separate piece of paper and then cut them out. Move them around until they all lie flat. The coloring of the letters is not significant in any way.

WINNING INNINGS (pages 16-17)

A base runner will be forced to move ahead as a new runner comes to his or her base. Watch out for runners who don't move ahead. All the small hits can be added together to make runs. In the seventh inning, the Sluggers scored two runs, while the Wonders scored only one. It may help to draw a baseball diamond and to use pennies for the runners.

HONEYCOMB (page 18)

The middle number is 4. The straight lines will be down or diagonal.

DIGIT DOES IT (pages 20-21)

The Audio Pirate are the final words in the message. Use the coded numbers in those words to help figure out the rest of the message.

THE ISSUE AT HAND (page 22)

A comic book's first anniversary issue is usually number 12. Since Monster Man appeared in the highest double-digit number with matching digits out of 36 issues, he was in book 33.

PLACES, EVERYONE (page 23)

From left to right, the tubes are labeled as follows:
hundred thousands, ten thousands, thousands, hundreds, tens, ones. Remember that the numbers in each tube will also be stacked in order from the smallest on the bottom to the largest on top.

LIQUID FUN (page 31)

Here is a list that shows how many ounces make up each measure:
1 cup = 8 ounces
1 pint = 16 ounces = 2 cups
1 quart = 32 ounces = 4 cups
1 gallon = 128 ounces = 16 cups

MYSTERIOUS TIMES (pages 32-33)

Each person is telling the truth. Look for someone who has time unaccounted for in the afternoon. To get your answer, be sure to add the time the suspects spent at each place and the time they spent traveling from one place to another.

SIDE ISSUE (page 35)

A pentagon is a figure with five sides. The triangle with the 15 in it is part of your solution.

HEY! EMERGENCY LOCATION PUZZLE SYSTEM (pages 38-39)

Use each city as the center of a circle. The circle goes out from the city for the given distance. For example, the line shown here goes out 100 miles from the city. Now draw an entire circle for each of the three cities at the given distance. The point where the circles of all three cities meet is the mystery city. It will help if you use a straight edge or a protractor to make your circles.

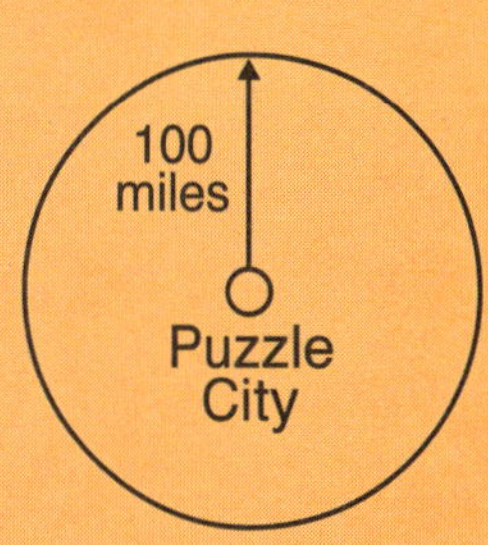

ANSWERS

COVER
256 + 111 + 408 + 121 + 104 = 1,000 pounds
All but the crate marked *317 pounds* can be sent at one time.

WORKING WORDS (page 3)
1. LADDER
2. SURPLUS
3. LESSON
4. NEVERMORE
5. DIVIDEND
6. SOMETIMES
7. OUTNUMBER
8. DESIGN
9. MALFUNCTION
10. DISCOUNT
11. COOPERATE
12. SETTLER

DRAGON AROUND (pages 4-5)
A. 1+2+3+3+3+2+3+3+2+2+2=26
B. 1+3+3+3+2+2+3+2+2+2+3+3=29
C. 1+2+2+3+3+2+3+3+2=21
D. 1+3+3+2+3+2+2+2+2+3+3+2=28

B needs the most people.

CARD QUEST (page 6)
The missing cards are the ace of hearts, seven of diamonds, eight of clubs, and the seven of spades. Delaware became the first state in 1787 (December 7).

OUT OF SHAPES (page 7)
What mathematical spell would a wizard cast to disappear?

A HEX-ALL-GONE!

BE SEATED (pages 8-9)

F1	F2	F3	F4	F5
W	R	I	T	E
E1	E2	E3	E4	E5
R	S	P	U	T
D1	D2	D3	D4	D5
W	O	R	D	S
C1	C2	C3	C4	C5
I	N	P	E	O
B1	B2	B3	B4	B5
P	L	E'	S	M
A1	A2	A3	A4	A5
O	U	T	H	S

Writers put words in people's mouths.

TAKE-OUT SERVICE (page 10)
Bag 9 – 2 = 7
Bag 16 – 8 = 8
Bag 26 – 7 =19
Bag 31 – 7 = 24
Bag 19 – 4 =15
Bag 22 – 6 = 16

COLOR BY NUMBERS (page 11)

DOT'S THE ANSWER (pages 12-13)
A. 7
T. 6
C. 2
E. 3
F. 4
H. 5
L. 13
N. 8
O. 1
S. 18
I. 16

This is the fastest bird with speeds of more than 200 miles per hour: FALCON.

This is the fastest land animal with speeds of up to 65 miles per hour: CHEETAH.

This is the fastest fish with speeds of up to 50 miles per hour: SAILFISH.

PACK IT IN (page 14)

Here is our answer. You may have found another.

BRIDGE MIX (page 15)

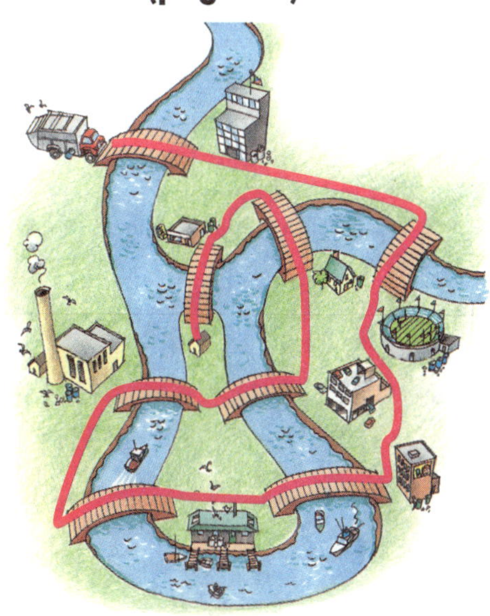

WINNING INNINGS (pages 16-17)

At the end of the sixth inning, the score was Wonders 5, Sluggers 3. The rest of the game was scored like this:

Inning	Sluggers	Wonders
6	3	5
7	2	1
8	3	0
9	1	4
Final score	9	10

Wonders won!

HONEYCOMB (page 18)

Here is our answer. You may have found another configuration.

SWIMMING SEQUENCES (page 19)

Len—7 (+1)
Ben—5 (alternating)
Lily—3 (–2)
Clarence—47 (double previous laps and add 1)
Mark—16 (+1, +2, +3, etc.)
Sally—6 (+1 to every other number)

DIGIT DOES IT (pages 20-21)

Avast, ye lubbers!
See these CDs? They are worth a small treasure. We have to ship them right away. Bring the discs to the West Side docks at midnight Friday.
The Audio Pirate

a–3	m–15
b–22	n–14
c–16	o–7
d–8	p–6
e–1	r–4
f–12	s–13
g–19	t–2
h–10	u–9
i–5	v–17
k–20	w–11
l–18	y–21

THE ISSUE AT HAND (page 22)

Gator Girl—12, 18
Monster Man—33
Beastly Ben—6
Greenteeth—5, 25
Dr. Somnambula—27

PLACES, EVERYONE (page 23)
897368
685247
333136

SCRAMBLED PICTURE (pages 24-25)

MATHMAGIC (page 26)
The two opposing sides of any die always add up to 7. I know that I just need to multiply the number of times rolled by 7 to get the answer. Each die was rolled twice, but there are two die, so I multiplied 7 by 4 to get 28.

HOT AND COLD (page 27)
A. 32° F
B. 60° F
C. 212° F
D. 98.6° F
E. 85° F
F. 102° F
G. 10° F

GET THE PICTURE (pages 28-29)
1. 12 × 10 = 120 Zoopnoodlers
2. 14 × 10 = 140 Frinkskis
3. 9 × 10 = 90 + 5 = 95 Allowichus
4. 6 × 10 = 60 + 5 = 65 Tricyclians
5. 18 × 10 = 180 Ignoradons
6. Ignoradons were seen most often.
7. Tricyclians were seen least often.
8. The cave painter saw 85 more Ignoradons than Allowichus.

PRECISE ICE (page 30)

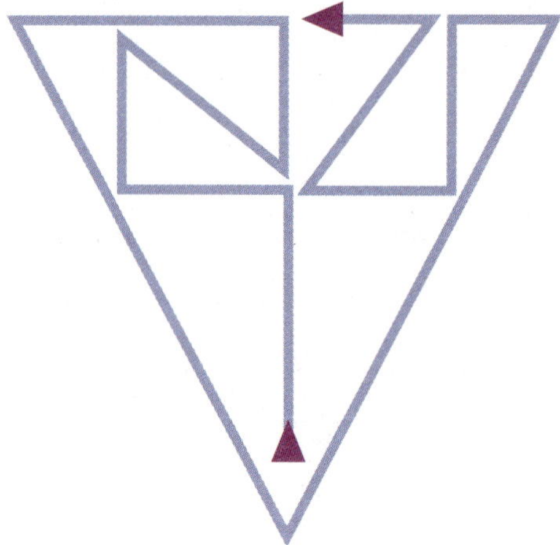

LIQUID FUN (page 31)
1. A gallon will fill a quart 4 times.
2. A gallon will fill a pint 8 times.
3. A pint will fill a cup 2 times.
4. A quart will fill a pint 2 times.
5. A gallon will fill a cup 16 times.

MYSTERIOUS TIMES (pages 32-33)
Cal Q. Later had enough time to steal the sculpture. He was at the post office at 3:50. The museum is only 15 minutes from there. He had plenty of time to get in and out of the museum by 5:00.

Maddox was at Cleo's at 4:31, which didn't leave enough time to reach the museum by 5:00. Ms. Vyde was at Ralph's at 5:08. Plicashun was at Tippy's Canoes at 4:35, not enough time to reach the museum before the heist.

TRY ANGLES (page 34)

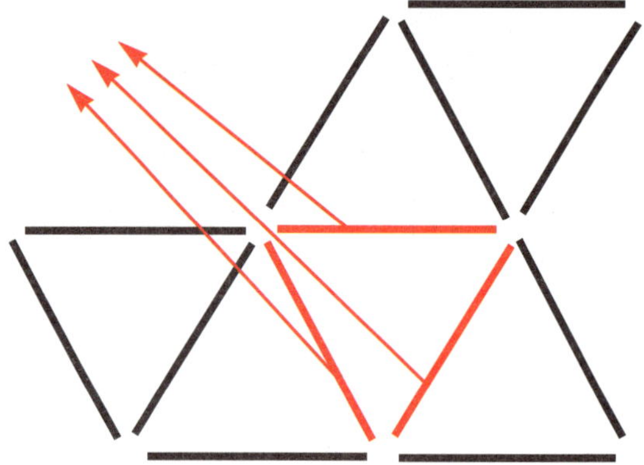